First published in Great Britain by HarperCollins Publishers Ltd in 1997

1 3 5 7 9 10 8 6 4 2

Copyright © 1997 Enid Blyton Company Ltd. Enid Blyton's signature mark and the word
'NODDY' are Registered Trade Marks of Enid Blyton Ltd.

ISBN: 0 00 198261-3

Cover design and illustrations by County Studios
A CIP catalogue record for this title is available from the British Library.

Printed and bound in Singapore by Imago.

NODDY™

CHRISTMAS STORYBOOK

Enid Blyton™

Collins

An Imprint of HarperCollins*Publishers*

THIS BOOK BELONGS TO

CONTENTS

A Letter from Noddy

Hallo, all you boys and girls!

I'm little Noddy. You all know me, don't you? I've got a nodding head and that's why I'm called Noddy. Would you like a head like that? I like mine.

I have a dear little car of my very own. I take my friends about in it – the Tubby Bears, who live next door to me, and Miss Fluffy Cat and Mr Jumbo and Mr Wobbly-Man and all the rest. My very best friend of all is Big-Ears. I do love him. He's a good friend because he always helps me when I get into trouble. He's a brownie, and he lives in his Toadstool House up in the woods.

You can share in our adventures and even meet Father Christmas in this very special story collection. I do hope you will like it. Wishing you all a very happy Christmas.

Love from *Noddy*

NODDY FEELS COLD

"Oh dear!" said Noddy, "I wanted to make a nice fire, because I'm so cold – but I've no firewood! Never mind, I'll go and ask Mrs Tubby Bear next door to give me some." So he went to knock at her door.

"Please Mrs Tubby, will you give me a little firewood?" asked Noddy.

"Yes, if you will do something for me," she said. "Go and ask Sally Skittle to let me have some mint out of her garden!" So away went Noddy to Sally Skittle's house.

"Please, Sally Skittle, may I pick some mint?" he asked.

"Well, you must do something for me!" said Sally. "Look – I've broken my teapot. I know Miss Fluffy Cat has two. You go and ask her to lend me one."

Noddy went to Miss Fluffy Cat's house and knocked at the door. She came to open it and smiled at Noddy.

"Please, Miss Fluffy Cat, would you lend me one of your teapots for Sally Skittle?" said Noddy.

"Well, you can take one of these," said Miss Fluffy Cat. "Which would you like – the big one or the small one?"

"The large one, please, because Sally has so many skittle children," said Noddy. "May I take it, Miss Fluffy Cat?"

"Well, do a little errand for me first," said Miss Fluffy Cat. "I want to borrow a ladder. So will you go to Mr Jumbo and ask for his? He always lends it to me when I want it."

"Oh dear!" said Noddy. "What a lot of errands I seem to be doing! And all because I want some firewood!"

He went to Mr Jumbo's. Mr Jumbo lived quite a long way away, down a long lane and over a hill.

And when Noddy got there, Mr Jumbo was out! But Mrs Jumbo was in, and was pleased to see Noddy.

"Oh, you want our ladder?" she said. "Certainly, Noddy – but b good little fellow, please, and go next door and ask Mrs Little Doll f some pegs for my clothes-line. I haven't enough."

So off Noddy went again, and asked Mrs Little Doll to lend him some pegs for Mrs Jumbo.

"Of course, Noddy," said Mrs Little Doll. "But please do something for me – take my dog and give him a little run, will you? I'm too busy today." So Noddy took her little dog and went for a walk with him. When they got back to Mrs Little Doll's house, they were quite out of breath.

"Thank you, Noddy! Here are the pegs," said Mrs Little Doll. Noddy took them and went back to Mrs Jumbo.

"Here are the pegs you wanted," he said. "Now may I please borrow your ladder, Mrs Jumbo?"

"There it is," said Mrs Jumbo, and off went Noddy with the big ladder – dear me, how heavy it was!

He took it to Miss Fluffy Cat's and she was pleased.

"Thank you, Noddy," she said. "Now here is the large teapot."

Noddy took the large teapot and carried it very carefully indeed to Sally Skittle's house.

"Thank you, Noddy," said Sally Skittle. "Go and pick some mint." So Noddy picked a nice bunch of mint and took it to Mrs Tubby Bear's. On his way, he smelt it – it really did smell nice and he put some in his button-hole. Soon he arrived at Mrs Tubby Bear's.

"Here is the mint," he said. "Is there enough?"

"Oh, plenty," said Mrs Tubby Bear. "Thank you, Noddy. Now what was it you said you wanted?"

"Some firewood, please," said Noddy, sitting down and mopping his head with his hanky.

"You *do* look hot, Noddy," said Mrs Tubby Bear. "Whatever have you been doing?"

"I've been rushing round all over the place!" said Noddy, "and I'm hot and out of breath!"

"Then why do you want to make yourself a fire?" asked Mrs Tubby Bear, giving him a bundle of wood.

"Oh dear – I don't think I do," said Noddy, giving it back. "I just want an ice-cream now, I'm so hot!" So off Noddy went to buy one. Funny little Noddy – wanting a fire and now going to buy an ice-cream!

NODDY AND THE LITTLE DOLLS

"Noddy – will you take my nine little doll children out for a picnic?" Mrs Jolly-Doll said to him one day. "They are very small, and could quite easily squeeze into your car. Take them to Windy Woods. It's nice there."

"I'd love to," said Noddy, who dearly loved a picnic. "We'll go tomorrow."

"I'll get the picnic basket ready," said Mrs Jolly-Doll. "And I'll put plenty in for you, too, kind little Noddy."

So next day Noddy went to fetch all the little dolls. They were very excited. Mrs Jolly-Doll helped them all into the car, and then put the picnic basket under Noddy's feet, which made it very awkward for him to drive.

"Oh dear – I'll have to drive with my knees knocking into my nose," said Noddy. "Now, are we all ready?"

"Noddy, please bring everyone back safely!" said Mrs Jolly-Doll. "There are ten of you. So, before you get into the car to come back, please count round and see that you have the right number. Can you count up to ten?"

"Oh *yes*," said Noddy. "One, two, three, four, five, six, seven, eight, nine, ten."

"Very clever," said Mrs Jolly-Doll. "Goodbye, and have a good time!"

Noddy drove off. He felt very happy. He liked the little dolls, and they liked him. He felt rather big, because they were so small, and it was very nice to feel big for a change.

They came to Windy Woods. Out they all got and had a game of hide-and-seek before lunch. Then Noddy undid the basket, and, my word, what a fine picnic they had! Egg sandwiches, tomato sandwiches, banana sandwiches. Chocolate biscuits, ginger biscuits. Fruit cake and ginger cake. Lemonade and orangeade. What a feast!

They played games again afterwards, but they all liked hide-and-seek best of all. Then Noddy asked a little bird the time.

"I don't know – except that it's time for you to go home," said the robin. "The sun is going down."

"Come along then, all of you!" cried little Noddy. "Get into the car. Oh, wait though. I must count you first to make sure that all ten of us are here!"

So he made the little dolls stand in a ring and he counted them. "One, two, three, four, five, six, seven, eight, nine. Oh my – there ought to be *ten* of us! Let me count again slowly. One-two-three-four-five-six-seven-eight-nine. There's only nine."

"Where's the tenth?" said a little doll, looking as if she were going to cry. "Is she lost at hide-and-seek?"

"She must be," said Noddy, and a great hunt began. But nobody else could be found. Noddy counted once more. "One, two, three, four, five, six, seven, eight, nine."

They all packed into his car, because by now it was getting dark. Noddy felt very upset. Whatever would Mrs Jolly-Doll say to him?

How dreadful to bring back only nine people, instead of ten.

They got to Mrs Jolly-Doll's house, and Mrs Jolly-Doll came out to welcome them. Noddy helped everyone out, feeling gloomier and gloomier. Oh dear – now he would *have* to tell Mrs Jolly-Doll the bad news.

"Mrs Jolly-Doll," he began. "I'm so very very sorry – but I'm afraid one of us is missing. I only counted nine, you see, instead of ten. But I'll go straight back to the woods and hunt all night long, I will really."

"You must have made a mistake in your counting, Noddy," said Mrs Jolly-Doll. "They all seem to be here."

"No, they're not. You listen to me counting them," said Noddy, and he stood the little dolls round him once more. "One, two, three, four, five, six, seven, eight, nine – there – one missing, you see!"

"But Noddy dear, you forgot to count *yourself!*" said Mrs Jolly-Doll. "See, *I'll* count you all – yourself, too. Listen. One, two, three, four, five, six, seven, eight, nine, TEN! And the tenth is you, little Noddy. You forgot to count yourself!"

"So I did," said Noddy, nodding and smiling. "So I did, aren't I SILLY!"

"Yes – but you're a darling!" said all the little dolls, and they hugged him so hard that he couldn't breathe.

Silly little Noddy! Fancy forgetting to count himself!

WHERE'S YOUR CAR, NODDY?

Now once Toyland was very jolly indeed, because Santa Claus had visited it in his beautiful sleigh. He had driven through it with his fine reindeer, and everyone cheered and clapped.

Santa Claus was the King of Toyland, and all the toys loved him. They put out hundreds of colourful flags. They danced and they sang in the market-place – you can see Noddy dancing with Big-Ears. And you can see Miss Fluffy Cat dancing with Mr Tubby Bear, having a wonderful time.

There were balloons everywhere, tied to the houses, and floating in the air like big coloured bubbles.

"Here come two big balloons, Noddy!" said Big-Ears. "Catch them, quick!"

So Noddy caught them. And then he caught four more, all bright colours and as pretty as could be.

"Tie them to your car, Noddy," said Big-Ears, "and I'll have two to make my bicycle look pretty, too."

Doesn't Noddy's car look fine?

Noddy went off with Big-Ears to get an ice-cream. While he was gone, a wind blew up the street – and it tugged at the balloons on Noddy's car. And, dear me, it tugged so hard that the balloons went up into the air – and took Noddy's car with them!

When Noddy and Big-Ears came back, there was no car to be seen!

"Where's my little car?" wailed Noddy.

"It went off with its balloons," said a skittle. "I saw it go. They floated away with it."

"I must find it, I must!" cried Noddy. "Big-Ears, let's get on your bicycle and go and find it."

On the way, they met two toy rabbits and Noddy asked, "Have you seen a car with balloons?"

"Yes," said the rabbits. "It went over towards the Noah's Ark. We watched it go and one of the balloons burst. You'd better go and find your car because more balloons might burst."

Off went Noddy and Big-Ears on the bicycle. They couldn't see the little car anywhere in the air.

And that wasn't surprising, because, as it floated along, two birds pecked at the balloons – and bang-pop! They all burst and the little car fell down beside the big Noah's Ark.

How surprised the animals were!

"What is it, dropping from the air?" said the bears.

"A car, a car!" cried the giraffe. "I'll drive it. I always wanted to drive a car!"

So the giraffe drove the car, and
then the bears wanted a turn.
As they raced up and down,
they bumped into the elephant,
who was very cross.

"Now then, now then!" he said,
and with his trunk he picked the two
naughty bears out of the car. He tried
to get in himself, but he bent it all to
one side, look! Oh, come quickly, Noddy, before the elephant breaks it
to bits!

Ring r-ring! Here come Noddy and Big-Ears on the bicycle. Noddy
gave such a yell at the elephant.

"What do you think you're doing? Get out at once!" Mr Noah heard
him shout and came out in surprise.

He ordered all the animals to go into the ark – here they go, two by
two – and then he helped Noddy and Big-Ears to put the car right.

"Would you give me a lift?" he said.

So Noddy gave him a lift to Toy Village, and Big-Ears followed on his bicycle.

"Will you stay in the car for a few minutes while I go and speak to Miss Fluffy Cat?" said Noddy to Mr Noah. And, will you believe it, while Noddy was gone, some balloons came bobbing by, near Mr Noah and he caught them and tied them to Noddy's car to make it look pretty. Well, well, well!

He just simply CAN'T understand why Noddy is so cross about it.

"*Silly* Mr Noah!" says Noddy. "I will NOT have balloons on my car any more!"

TESSIE BEAR'S LITTLE STAR

"Tessie dear – go and fetch a pail of water," said Tessie's Auntie Bear one night. "I've spilt some jam on the kitchen floor and I really must wash it off."

Tessie went out into the garden to fetch a pail of water. She let the bucket down into the well, and pulled it up, quite full.

She set it down on the ground – and then looked up at the sky. It was FULL of stars!

"Aren't they pretty?" said little Tessie to herself. "I'd like a necklace of stars. I wonder if any of them ever fall down? I might find one then."

And do you know, JUST as she looked at the starry sky, a bright star rushed down it – and disappeared!

"It left its place! It ran all down the sky! It was the loveliest shooting star I've ever seen!" said Tessie. "I wonder where it fell? Oh, I DO wish I could find it!"

She turned to pick up her bucket – and then how she stared!

"Why! There's a star twinkling up at me from the water!" she cried. "There is, there is! Oh, you dear little star, did you fall into my pail? You must have! One minute you were in the sky – and the next I see you here!"

She looked at the star twinkling in the pail.

"Oh, I can't take you indoors and empty you out on a dirty floor," she said. "I'll catch you in my hand and take you to Noddy. He will like you."

So she put in her hand but of course she couldn't catch the star. That wasn't surprising, because it was only a big star's reflection in the water! Tessie didn't know that.

She picked up the heavy bucket and went to the gate. She meant to walk all the way to Noddy's house with the star in it! Away she went, staggering down the road because the pail was so heavy.

And then Mr Toy-Dog came hurrying up the street and bumped into her – and over went the pail! Splish-splash! Out poured the water!

"Sorry!" called Mr Toy-Dog. "But why carry pails of water at night?"

Tessie Bear was very, very sad. She hunted everywhere for the shining star she had carried in the pail, but she couldn't find it anywhere! She sat down on the kerb and cried.

She wasn't very far from Noddy's house, so she thought she would go and tell him what had happened. Noddy heard a timid little knocking at his door and went to open it. How pleased he was to see little Tessie Bear!

"Come in, Tessie," he said. "But goodness me, why are you carrying an empty pail?"

"When it was full, it had a star in it, Noddy, a star that fell out of the sky," said Tessie. "It was so pretty that I wanted to give it to you."

"Why? For a pet?" said Noddy. "Oh, fancy keeping a star for a pet! Tessie, you are very sweet to come all the way here to bring me a star for a present. But it isn't here – the pail's empty."

"Someone bumped into me and spilt all the water, and the star must have fallen out – I couldn't find it," said Tessie, and she burst into tears again.

Well, Noddy gave her some cocoa and some sugar biscuits and she soon cheered up. Then he took her home and filled her pail at the well again for her.

"Oh look!" he said, when the pail came up full of water again, "LOOK, Tessie – the star is there after all, twinkling away like anything!"

So it was! Noddy darted his hand into the water and tried to catch hold of the star twinkling there – but at that very moment the sky began to cloud over, and hide all the stars. The big black cloud hid the star whose reflection had shone in the water – and because Noddy could no longer see it in the pail, he was sure he must have caught it in his hand. He put it into his pocket at once.

"There, Tessie, I've got it!" he said. "Now you go indoors and don't cry any more. I'll keep your star for ever and ever!"

Do *you* want to see the star that twinkled in Tessie's pail? Then fill a bucket with water on the next starry night, and look down into it. There will be a star there for you too!

NODDY IS QUITE CLEVER

Once when Noddy went to tea with Mrs Tubby, the toy cat was there. Her name was Miss Tibby, and she was quite one of the nicest of the toy cats.

"Good afternoon, Miss Tibby," said Noddy politely. "I hope you're well."

"She's feeling a bit upset," said Mrs Tubby. "She's just discovered a funny thing. She has fine claws in her front paws – but none in her back ones."

"Oh," said Noddy. "Does it matter?"

"Of course it does," said Miss Tibby. "I don't feel a proper toy cat without claws in all my feet. I never noticed it before. One of the dolls laughed at me this morning, and told me, and I was most upset."

"Can't you *buy* claws?" said Noddy.

"You're silly," said the toy cat, and wiped her eyes.

"But you wear shoes," said Noddy. "How did the doll see you hadn't claws?"

"I went to try on some new sandals," said Miss Tibby, "and she noticed when she was trying sandals on my feet. Really, I was dreadfully upset."

"She won't even eat any tea, and I've baked such a lovely chocolate cake," said Mrs Tubby. "I think I won't cut it today, if you are sure you won't have any, Miss Tibby. I'll keep it for tomorrow."

Noddy didn't like hearing that a bit, because he knew he wasn't going to tea with Mrs Tubby tomorrow. It meant he wouldn't have a piece of the lovely cake.

He sat staring mournfully out into Mrs Tubby's pretty little garden.

The roses were out, and looked beautiful. And then, quite suddenly, Noddy's face began beaming, and he stood up.

"Please can I get down for a minute?" he said. "I've thought of an idea."

He went out into the garden to the rose-trees. He looked at each one. He chose one that had very very sharp prickles all the way down the stem.

"You'll do nicely," he said. He broke off ten sharp curved thorns, and took them carefully back to Mrs Tubby's house.

"What *have* you been doing?" asked Mrs Tubby. "Smelling every rose, I should think!"

"I've brought something for Miss Tibby," said Noddy, and he put the curved prickles on her plate. "Claws! Fine, sharp, scratchy claws, just like the ones she has in her front paws. Would they do for your back paws, Miss Tibby?"

"*Well,*" said Miss Tibby in astonishment, "what wonderful claws! Where did you buy them?"

"I didn't," said Noddy. "I broke them off Mrs Tubby's rose-trees. You don't mind, do you, Mrs Tubby?"

"Not a bit. Why, you can be quite clever, Noddy!" said Mrs Tubby. "Look, I am going to cut you a very very very big slice of my chocolate cake; just because I am so pleased with you!"

So Miss Tibby got her claws and Noddy got his chocolate cake, and they were both very happy.

NODDY AND THE WOODEN HORSE

Now once when Noddy was driving along a country road, his car suddenly made a peculiar noise, and then stopped.

"Good gracious! What's wrong with you?" said Noddy, in alarm, and he got out to see. "Your wheels haven't got a puncture, and you've plenty of petrol. Then WHY don't you go?"

"Parp-parp," said the car, dolefully, and gave a little rattle.

"I'll have to take you to the garage and get you mended," said Noddy. "Something has gone wrong. But dear me, I'll have to push you all the way because this is a very lonely road and there's nobody to help me."

So he began to push and push, and how he panted and puffed.

"I sound like an engine going up a hill!" said Noddy. "Oh dear, I shall never get you to the garage!"

He pushed the car round the corner of the lane, and then he

suddenly heard a noise. "Hrrrrumph! Help! Hrrrrumph!"

"Now what can *that* be?" said Noddy, and he stood and listened.

"Nay-hay-hay-hay-hay! Hrrrrumph! Help!"

"Why – it's a horse in trouble!" said Noddy, and he squeezed through the hedge to find it. Sure enough, in the field beyond was a small horse, neighing and snorting loudly.

"What's the matter?" called Noddy.

"I walked into this muddy bit," said the horse, "and look – my front legs have sunk down into the mud and I can't get them out!"

Noddy ran to help him. "I'll pull you out!" he said. "What part of you shall I pull?"

"My tail," said the horse. "It's a very strong tail. Hold hard – pull. PULL! Pull HARDER. I'm coming. I'm coming!"

Noddy pulled hard at the wooden horse's tail, and, quite suddenly, the horse's front legs came out of the mud, and the horse sat down hard on Noddy.

"Oooh, don't!" said Noddy. "I'm squashed to nothing. Get up, wooden horse. Don't sit on me like this."

"Sorry," said the horse, and got up. "You really are very kind. It was lucky for me that you came by just then in your car."

"Yes, it was," said Noddy. "But I wasn't *in* my car. Something's gone wrong with it, and I've got to push it all the way into Toyland Village. Goodness, I shall be tired!"

"You needn't be," said the wooden horse. "I am quite used to pulling carts. I could pull your car for you, if you like, all the way to the garage! I'd be glad to do you a good turn, little Noddy."

"Oh *thank* you!" said Noddy. "How lucky I am! Come along – I'll get my ropes and tie you to the car. What fun!"

So off they went with Noddy sitting in his car, steering it carefully, and the little wooden horse walking in front, pulling it well. How everyone stared!

"Aren't I lucky?" called little Noddy. "My car broke down – and I found a little wooden horse to pull it!"

"You *are* lucky, Noddy – but, you see, you're kind too, and kind people are *always* lucky!"

NODDY AND THE RED GOBLINS

"Listen, Noddy – if you go through the Goblin Wood in the evening, DON'T stop, whatever happens!" said Big-Ears.

" Oh. But why ever not?" said Noddy, surprised.

"Because the red goblins are about again and you know what tricks they get up to," said Big-Ears. "They'd love to have your car, Noddy – so DO NOT stop for anything if you go through the Goblin Wood."

"But suppose someone hails me and wants to be taken somewhere?" said Noddy.

"Don't stop even for that," said Big-Ears. "It may be a trick."

"All right," said Noddy. "But it does seem rather silly, Big-Ears."

"Now *you're* being rather silly, Noddy," said Big-Ears, crossly. "I'm only trying to help you."

Well, Noddy was very good. He did as Big-Ears told him, and whenever he drove through the Goblin Wood for anything he wouldn't stop for a moment, no matter how the goblins tried to make him.

First they pretended that they wanted to hire his car, and they stood by the roadside, signalling to him – but he drove straight on.

Then two of them walked right in the very middle of the road, thinking *that* would make him stop. But Noddy drove top speed at them, yelling out loudly, "Look out, LOOK OUT, I can't stop,

I CAN'T STOP!"

And the two red goblins hopped out of the way very quickly indeed. They were very angry because they couldn't get Noddy to stop. They did so badly want his car.

Then they thought of a good trick.

"Look!" said one. "I'll blow up this paper bag – and, just as Noddy goes by, I'll hide behind a tree and pop it – BANG – and he'll think he's got a puncture and stop to see."

"Oh good – then we'll all rush out and take his car and go off in it!" said another.

Well, it was a very good trick indeed. Noddy came along quite fast in his car that evening, keeping a sharp look-out for the goblins – but he didn't see a single one.

They were all well hidden! One of them was behind a tree close to the road, and when he heard Noddy's car coming, he blew up his big paper bag – and then he popped it – BANG!

Noddy was just driving by, and he put on his brakes at once and stopped. "Goodness – that sounded like a puncture in one of my tyres!" he said, and got out to see. He forgot all about Big-Ears' warning.

In a trice the red goblins were on him. They rolled him in the dust and then they clambered into the car, and away they went, leaving little Noddy howling all by himself!

"Big-Ears, oh Big-Ears, why didn't I remember what you said," wept poor Noddy, getting up and beginning to walk down the long, long road.

It took him a good time to get to Big-Ears' Toadstool House, and he was crying bitterly when he knocked at the door.

Big-Ears opened it, and Noddy went inside. "Oh, Big-Ears, I stopped on the Goblin Wood road – I thought I had a puncture but I hadn't – and all the goblins rolled me in the dust and drove away in my little car. Oh Big-Ears, I'm so-o-o-o miserable!" Big-Ears put his arms round Noddy.

"I've been waiting for you to come to me," he said. "I knew you'd be along sooner or later."

"How did you know?" wept Noddy. "Oh, Big-Ears, my dear little car will be so unhappy. It will never come back. I'll never see it again. Oh, those wicked red goblins, I wish they could be punished."

Big-Ears laughed. "Don't you worry!" he said. "They have been punished already. Badly punished. And your little car is quite all right."

"Oh, Big-Ears – how do you know all this?" cried Noddy, surprised. "Who told you? What's happened?"

"I'll tell you what has happened," said Big-Ears, "but please stop crying tears all down my waistcoat, or else I really must get an umbrella. Cheer up, Noddy!"

"I'm cheering up," said Noddy, and he gave Big-Ears a very small smile. "Now, tell me."

"Well, your little car was very, very angry when the goblins drove it away," said Big-Ears. "So instead of driving off to their town as they wanted it to, it drove itself straight to the big duck-pond – and it stopped right on the very edge – and all the goblins shot straight up into the air and fell SPLASH into the water!"

"Oh! Oh, isn't my car clever!" cried Noddy, and he laughed and laughed. "What a shock for the red goblins! What happened next?"

"Nothing much except that the car came straight here to wait for you," said Big-Ears. "It's outside now, but you were crying so much you didn't see it. Call it!"

"Car! Little car!" shouted Noddy in delight. And from outside came the sound Noddy knew so well.

"Parp-parp! Parp-parp-parp!"

Well done, little car – you deserve a very good polish all over – and Noddy will see that you get it!

HO-HO-HO-HO!

One morning, when Noddy had driven the farmer's wife to market and back, she gave him twelve new-laid eggs for himself.

"Oooh, thank you!" said Noddy. "I do so like an egg for breakfast! There's enough here for Tessie Bear too."

But Tessie was away, so Noddy thought he would share them with old Big-Ears. He drove up to the Toadstool House and knocked at the door.

No one opened it. Bother! Big-Ears must be out. Noddy opened the door and went in. No – Big-Ears was there – but he was fast asleep in his chair, quite tired out with all the gardening he had done!

He had put his hat on the table beside him, and taken off his shoes. Noddy smiled and was careful not to nod his head in case his bell rang and wakened Big-Ears.

"I'll give him a nice surprise," thought Noddy. "I'll pop six eggs inside his hat – and when he wakes up, he *will* be pleased to see them! He can fry some for his dinner."

So Noddy carefully put six of the biggest eggs into Big-Ears' hat, and then tiptoed out of the room. Away he went in his car, thinking how surprised Big-Ears would be to find eggs inside his hat.

Big-Ears woke up at last – and jumped up at once when he saw how late it was. He caught up his red hat and jammed it on his head...

Ooooooh! Whatever was this trickling all down his neck? Big-Ears put up his hand to feel – and his fingers came away covered with yellow egg-yolk! He tore off his hat and looked inside.

"Eggs! Eggs in my hat! All smashed to bits when I put it on my head! Look at it – and look at my clothes! COVERED with yellow egg-yolks! Ruined! Who did this?

WHO DID IT, I say! Wait till I get hold of him! I'll complain to Mr
Plod! I'll go this very minute!"

But poor Big-Ears couldn't go in his eggy clothes.
They looked dreadful, and were sticky with
yolk wherever he touched them. So he
took them off and put on
a clean set of clothes.
Away he went on his
bicycle, with no hat, as
angry as could be. Wait till
Mr Plod hears about this!
Perhaps it was that bad little
Tricky Teddy who had
played such a trick.

Now Noddy had to go past Big-Ears'
house in the afternoon, on his way back from Rocking-Horse Town.

"I'll just pop in and see if he liked the eggs," he said. "Perhaps
he will ask me to tea."

So in he went – and the very first thing he saw was Big-Ears' hat, all
messed with broken eggs. Then he saw Big-Ears' other clothes on the
ground, all yellow and sticky too. Noddy sat down suddenly in a chair,
feeling very scared. He guessed at once what had happened.

"Oh DEAR! I never thought he'd put his hat on without looking
inside. Oh DEAR, DEAR, DEAR! Now I'm going to get into terrible
trouble. Oh, I'm so sorry, so very sorry. What shall I do?"

Then an idea came to him. He picked up the eggy hat and clothes, and drove home with them as fast as ever he could. He meant to wash them at once, and get them clean for poor old Big-Ears.

My goodness, how well he washed them! Soon he was pegging them out on the line in the wind, and then went indoors to make some tea – and at that very minute he heard the sound of Big-Ears' bicycle bell!

"Oh – now he's going to be so cross!" said poor Noddy, and opened the door to let in Big-Ears. Big-Ears began to tell him at once about the eggs.

"I've been to Mr Plod," he said, "and told him I'm sure it was Tricky Teddy, and..."

And then he looked out of the window and saw all his clothes dancing about in the wind on Noddy's line! He was so surprised that he couldn't say a word!

"Oh Big-Ears, dear Big-Ears, I put the eggs into your hat for a *present*," said Noddy. "And I was DREADFULLY sorry when I saw what had happened. So I took all your things back to wash. Please, please, Big-Ears, don't take me to Mr Plod."

Well, Big-Ears didn't. He stared at little Noddy as he spoke – and then his face wrinkled up, and his mouth opened wide – and out came the biggest laugh that Noddy had ever heard!

"HO-HO-HO-HO-HO! I might have guessed! HO-HO-HO-HO! Who else but you would be so kind and so SILLY, Noddy! You'll make me die of laughing, you really will! HO-HO-HO-HO-HO!"

A Hole in his Pocket

"Oh dear!" said Noddy, "I do believe there's a teeny little hole in my pocket! Yes, there is. I *must* remember to mend it. I'll do it after my breakfast."

But he didn't. He felt the hole again and thought that really it was so very small nothing could fall through it.

"I'll mend you tonight, hole," said Noddy. But the hole didn't stay small. It grew bigger, and when Noddy began to put sixpences and shillings into his pocket, as passengers paid him for riding in his little car, the hole grew bigger still.

Noddy forgot all about it. He felt very very pleased with himself as he drove home that evening. He jingled his money and made up his mind to go and buy little Tessie Bear and dear old Big-Ears a present each the very next day.

When he got home he washed himself, and sat down to a very late tea. How hungry he was! He ate all the cakes in his tin, and half a loaf of bread, and butter and honey.

"And now I'll go and dig my garden," he said. "I feel just like digging. Where's my spade?"

Well, he dug and he dug, and grew very hot indeed. Mrs Tubby Bear looked over the fence and laughed.

"You're as red as one of the apples on my tree!" she said. "Come over and pick one, and tell me your news while you have a rest."

Noddy was pleased. He went into Mrs Tubby Bear's garden, and picked himself a fine apple. Then he sat down to tell her his news.

"I had a very, very busy day, Mrs Tubby Bear," he said. "And I made a lot of money!"

"Did you now?" said Mrs Tubby Bear, going on with her knitting. "And what are you going to spend it on?"

"Well, tomorrow, the very first thing I shall do is to buy Big-Ears a new book to read," said Noddy. "He's read his old one eighty-two times, he says – so it's time he had a new one, isn't it?"

"It certainly is," said Mrs Tubby.

"And then I'm going to buy little Tessie Bear a jar of honey," said Noddy. "She loves honey. All bears do. Did you know that, Mrs Tubby?"

"Well, yes, I did," said Mrs Tubby, smiling. "You see, I've been a bear myself for a very long time, Noddy."

"Oh yes. I forgot," said Noddy. "Well, you are so very nice, Mrs Tubby, that I shall buy *you* a present too. Let me count my money – then you'll see what a lot I've got." He put his hand into his pocket – and then he gave such a howl that Mrs Tubby almost dropped her knitting.

"My money! It's gone!" cried Noddy, and tears began to run down his cheeks. "I had a hole in my pocket, and I didn't mend it. My money has dropped out, every bit of it. Now I shan't be able to buy *anyone* a present."

"Oh, Noddy, Noddy, you little silly!" said Mrs Tubby. "But surely you would have *heard* it drop out, clinkity-clink? Yes, surely you would."

"I didn't, I didn't," wept Noddy. "Oh, why didn't I?"

"Well then – the money must have dropped on something so soft that you didn't hear it," said Mrs Tubby. "On a soft carpet – or grass – or... OH! I know where your money will be, Noddy!"

"Where?" asked Noddy, wiping his eyes.

"Where you were *digging*, of course!" said Mrs Tubby. "It must have dropped out then; every time you drove your spade into the ground you must have jerked out money! And you didn't hear it because it fell into the soft earth!"

"Oh, Mrs Tubby – you *are* clever!" said Noddy. "I'll go and look, now, at once, this very minute!"

And over the wall he went into his own little garden. There in the earth, just as Mrs Tubby said, was every bit of his money! Oh, how happy Noddy was! He picked it all up – and put it into his pocket!

But that was silly, wasn't it! Mrs Tubby scolded him. "There you go again, little Noddy, using that hole in your pocket! Fetch a needle and cotton, come back here, and I'll mend it for you!"

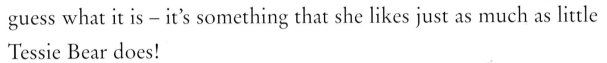

So now it's mended and his money is safe – and the very *first* present he buys tomorrow morning is going to be for Mrs Tubby! You can guess what it is – it's something that she likes just as much as little Tessie Bear does!

(*Noddy says, if you're not very clever at guessing, well, it rhymes with* MONEY)

FATHER CHRISTMAS
COMES TO TOYLAND

One morning Big-Ears came knocking at Noddy's little front door in great excitement.

"I've got some very exciting news, Noddy," said Big-Ears. "Father Christmas is coming next week in his sleigh, with four reindeer. He's staying the night with my brother, Little-Ears."

"Goodness! What an honour!" said Noddy, feeling very excited too. "Shall I be able to see Father Christmas?"

"Well, my brother, Little-Ears, has asked me to his house on the night that Father Christmas is there," said Big-Ears, "and I thought you could take me in your car, Noddy, and sing a song outside the house while Father Christmas is having his supper!"

"Oh, Big-Ears! Oh, what a wonderful idea!" said Noddy, almost falling off his chair in excitement. "Oh, I'll make my car look simply beautiful."

At last the big day arrived and everyone was up very early. Noddy gave his car one last polish. It really looked magnificent. He tied a big bow in front, in the middle of the bumper.

The car was so pleased with itself, it hooted, "Parp-parp-PARP!"

Noddy took off his overall and went to wash himself and dress. He even polished up the bell on the top of his blue hat.

The roadway had to be cleared for Father Christmas' arrival, because the sleigh and the four reindeer took up rather a lot of room. Noddy put his car safely in the garage, but he left the door open so that the car could join in the excitement and hoot at the right time.

Noddy went to stand at his gateway and Big-Ears came along on his bicycle.

The noise of the bells grew louder and louder. JING-JING-JING-JINGLE-JING! JINGLE-JING! And then Noddy saw the reindeer coming up the road. How lovely they looked with their great antlers growing from their heads! JING-JING-JINGLE-JING. And there was Father Christmas in his sleigh, smiling all over his big red face, and his blue eyes twinkling all the time. He waved his hand to everyone, and his red cloak flew out in the wind behind him.

Noddy gave a big sigh.

"Never mind," said Big Ears, "you might get a peep at him tonight, but that's all, little Noddy. He's a Most Important Person, you know."

"Yes, I do know. It's what my song says," said little Noddy, his head nodding up and down. "I'm glad my song is going to be sung outside Little-Ears' house tonight."

That evening Mr Tubby arranged the singers in a row. Noddy stood in the front, suddenly feeling very shy. Everyone looked at him, and

Noddy raised a little twig he had found in a ditch.

"OH...!" sang everyone, and then went on with the song.

"There's a Most Important Person

That I hope we're going to see..."

Right on to the end of the song they all went, and you should have heard how they shouted out Father Christmas' name when they came to it in the song!

The door opened – and out came the Most Important Person himself!

He smiled round at everyone and his blue eyes twinkled brightly.

"Very nice indeed," he said. "And may I ask which of you wrote that extremely good song?"

"Noddy did," said Miss Fluffy, and she pushed Noddy towards Father Christmas. "He's our taxi-driver and he often makes up songs."

"Dear me – so this is little Noddy!" said Father Christmas. He put out his hand and Noddy shook it, very red in the face.

"So you're a taxi-driver, are you?" said Father Christmas. "Where's your car?"

"Here," said Noddy, finding his tongue, and waved his hand towards his little car.

"Parp-parp," said the car, and put its lights on and off all by itself.

"What a dear little car!" said Father Christmas. "And how beautifully clean and shiny! Dear me, I wish I could travel through Toyland in this instead of going in my bumpy old sleigh."

"Oh," said Noddy, going even redder than ever, "please have my car while you are here in Toyland. It's very easy to drive."

"That's kind of you," said Father Christmas, "but it would be a change for me to be driven instead of driving myself. I suppose you wouldn't like to come with me and drive me where I want to go?"

Noddy lost his tongue again. He couldn't say a single word! He just stared at Father Christmas as if he couldn't believe his ears.

"Oh," said Noddy, sitting down suddenly. "Oh! I must be dreaming!" But he wasn't – it was quite, quite true!

Next morning Noddy was outside Little-Ears' house at exactly nine o'clock. Out came Father Christmas.

"Now, let me see," he said, taking out a fat notebook. "I want to go to Bouncing Ball Village. I hear that some of the balls I gave to the children last year hadn't got much bounce in them. I must enquire into that."

Off they went, Noddy feeling as proud as could be. His bell jingled all the time.

"You sound like a small reindeer, jingling like that!" said Father Christmas, and gave one of his enormous laughs.

"Hallo – are we in Bouncing Ball Village so soon? Good. Call the Chief Bouncer to me, will you?"

Little balls came bouncing round to see who had come. When they saw it was Father Christmas they bounced in excitement, trying to jump right over the car.

The Chief Bouncer was an enormous coloured ball, the kind that likes to be played with at the seaside. He listened to Father Christmas and then he promised to see that every ball in the village should have proper bouncing lessons before being sent to the world of boys and girls.

"Now go to Teddy Town," said Father Christmas. "I've had very good reports from boys and girls about their teddy bears – they love them very much. I want to give some praise there."

On they went to Teddy Town. The Chief Teddy was very proud to see Father Christmas.

"You are training your teddy bears well," said Father Christmas. "I am pleased with you. One little girl has asked for a tiny doll's house teddy bear. Can you do anything about that?"

"Certainly, Father Christmas," said the Chief Teddy.

On they went, and the little car behaved beautifully. It didn't knock any lamp-posts down, it didn't go into any puddles, and it ran round bumps in the road instead of jolting over them.

It was a very exciting day. Noddy felt so proud to be driving Father Christmas. He felt prouder still to be sitting at a table and having tea with him, and he was very pleased to find that Father Christmas liked ice-creams as much as he did!

They slept in Humming-Top Village that night, and all night long there was the humming of excited tops who couldn't go to sleep because Father Christmas had come to visit them.

Next day off they went again. They went to Wooden-Engine Village, and Noddy had time to drive one. He had always wanted to do that. And he was so excited that he really drove it much too fast!

Noddy was very sorry when it was time to go home.

"We'll have a party when we get back," Father Christmas said to Noddy. "I feel like a party, Noddy. Do you?"

"Oh, yes – I always feel like a party – just like I always feel like an ice-cream," said Noddy.

Big-Ears was very pleased to see Noddy safely home again and to hear from Father Christmas what a splendid little driver he had been.

"We're going to have a party," said Noddy. "Will you and Little-Ears arrange it, Big-Ears?"

"You shall have one tomorrow!" said Big-Ears, beaming. "In the market-place, so that everyone can come. I'll get the big town-bell and go and call out the news."

"DINGA-DONG! DINGA-DONG! News! NEWS! NEWS!"

Well, it wasn't long before everyone heard the news that Father Christmas and little Noddy were safely back and were going to have a party. Goodness me, what excitement there was!

The reindeer were asked to the party, too, and Little-Ears spent a long time polishing their antlers for them. In fact, everyone was asked, even the bunnies in the woods.

The party began at three o'clock, and there was so much to eat that the tables that stood in the middle of the market-place creaked under the weight of it all.

Father Christmas sat at the top of the table and Noddy sat on his right-hand-side, feeling so proud that he could hardly speak a word.

But his bell rang all the time, and his little car, parked nearby, hooted.

"Jingle-parp, parp-jingle-jing, parple, parple-parple, jingle-jing!"

Father Christmas got up and made a speech.

"I don't make long speeches," he said, "but I do want to say that Noddy is one of the nicest, kindest little toys I've ever met, and quite the best driver!"

"Hooray! Hooray!" cried everyone.

"Speech, Noddy, speech!" shouted Mr and Mrs Tubby. Noddy began to tremble. "I don't know what to say," said little Noddy. "I-I don't-know-" And suddenly he stood up straight and smiled.

"It's all right!" he said. "I'll sing a song instead!"

And here is the song that he sang at that wonderful party:

> "I'm only little Noddy
> Who's got a song to sing,
> And a little car to ride in,
> And a bell to jingle-jing.
> I've a little house to live in
> And a little garage too.
> But I've something BIG inside me,
> And that's my love for YOU –
> My love for ALL of you!"

Much better than a speech, little Noddy. No wonder everyone is clapping and cheering you. Well done!